Victor

GW01158170

Lester Del Rey

Alpha Editions

This edition published in 2024

ISBN : 9789362929396

Design and Setting By
Alpha Editions
www.alphaedis.com
Email - info@alphaedis.com

VICTORY

It seemed Earth was a rich, and undefended planet in a warring, hating galaxy. Things can be deceptive though; children playing can be quite rough—but that ain't war, friend!

BY LESTER del REY

I

From above came the sound of men singing. Captain Duke O'Neill stopped clipping his heavy black beard to listen. It had been a long time since he'd heard such a sound—longer than the time since he'd last had a bath or seen a woman. It had never been the singing type of war. Yet now even the high tenor of old Teroini, who lay on a pad with neither legs nor arms, was mixed into the chorus. It could mean only one thing!

As if to confirm his thoughts, Burke Thompson hobbled past the cabin, stopping just long enough to shout. "Duke, we're home! They've sighted Meloa!"

"Thanks," Duke called after him, but the man was hobbling out of sight, eager to carry the good news to others.

Fourteen years, Duke thought as he dragged out his hoarded bottle of water and began shaving. Five since he'd seen Ronda on his last leave. Now the battered old wreck that was left of the flagship was less than an hour from home base, and the two other survivors of the original fleet of eight hundred were limping along behind. Three out of eight hundred—but they'd won! Meloa had her victory.

And far away, Earth could rest in unearned safety for a while.

Duke grimaced bitterly. It was no time to think of Earth now. He shucked off his patched and filthy clothes and reached for the dress grays he had laid out in advance; at least they were still in good condition, almost unused. He dressed slowly, savoring the luxury of clean clothes. The buttons gave him trouble; his left hand looked and behaved almost like a real one, but in the three years since he got it, there had been no chance to handle buttons.

Then he mastered the trick and stepped back to study the final results. He didn't look bad. Maybe a little gaunt and in need of a good haircut. But his face hadn't aged as much as he had thought. The worst part was the pasty white where his beard had covered his face, but a few days under Meloa's sun would fix that. Maybe he could spend a month with Ronda at a beach. He still had most of his share of his salary—nearly a quarter million Meloan credits; even if the rumors of inflation were true, that should be enough.

He stared at his few possessions, then shrugged and left them. He headed up the officers' lift toward the control room, where he could see Meloa swim into view and later see the homeport of Kordule as they landed.

The pilot and navigator were replacements, sent out to bring the old ship home, and their faces showed none of the jubilation of the crew. They nodded at him as he entered, staring toward the screens without expression. Aside from the blueness of their skins and the complete absence of hair, they looked almost human, and Duke had long since stopped thinking of them as anything else.

"How long?" he asked.

The pilot shrugged. "Half an hour, captain. We're too low on fuel to wait for clearance, even if control is working. Don't worry. There'll be plenty of time to catch the next ship to Earth."

"Earth?" Duke glowered at him, suspecting a joke, but there was no humor on the blue face. "I'm not going back!" Then he frowned. "What's an Earth ship doing on Meloa?"

The navigator exchanged a surprised look with the pilot, and nodded as if some signal had passed between them. His voice was as devoid of expression as his face. "Earth resumed communication with us the day the truce was signed," he answered. He paused, studying Duke. "They're giving free passage back to Earth to all terran veterans, captain."

Nice of them, Duke thought. They were willing to let the men who'd survived come back, just as they hadn't forbidden anyone to go. Very nice! They could keep their world—and all the other coward planets like them! When the humanoid world of Meloa had been attacked by the insectile monsters from Throm, Earth could have ended the invasion in a year, as those with eyes to see had urged her. But she hadn't chosen to do so. Instead, she had stepped back on her high retreat of neutrality, and let the Throm aliens do as they liked. It wasn't the first time she'd acted like that, either.

With more than half of the inhabited planets occupied by various monsters, it seemed obvious that the humanoid planets had to make a common stand. If Meloa fell, it would be an alien stepping stone that could lead back eventually to Earth itself. And once the monsters realized that Earth was unwilling to fight, her vast resources would no longer scare them—she'd be only a rich plum, ripe for the plucking.

When Duke had been one of the first to volunteer for Meloa, he had never realized his home world could refuse to join the battle. He'd believed in Earth and humanity then. He'd waited through all the grim days when it seemed Throm must win—when the absence of replacements proved the communiques from Meloa to be nothing but hopeful lies. But there had been no help. Earth's neutrality remained unshaken.

And now, after fourteen years in battle hell, helping to fight off a three-planet system of monsters that might have swarmed against all the humanoid races, Earth was willing to forgive him and take him back to the shame of his birthright!

"I'm staying," he said flatly. "Unless you Meloans want to kick me out now?"

The pilot swung around, dropping a quick hand on his shoulder. "Captain," he said, "that isn't something to joke about. We won't forget that there would be no Meloa today without men like you. But we can't ask you to stay. Things have changed—insanely. The news we sent to the fleet was pure propaganda!"

"We guessed that," Duke told him. "We knew the Throm ships. And when the dispatches reported all those raids without any getting through, we stopped reading them. How many did penetrate, anyhow?"

"Thirty-one full raids," the navigator said woodenly. "Thirty-one in the last four months!"

"*Thirty-one!* What happened to the home fleet?"

"We broke it up and sent it out for your replacements," the pilot answered dully. "It was the only chance we had to win."

Duke swallowed the idea slowly. He couldn't picture a planet giving up its last protection for a desperate effort to end the war on purely offensive drive. Three billion people watching the home fleet take off, knowing the skies were open for all the hell that a savage enemy could send! On Earth, the World Senate hadn't permitted the building of one battleship, for fear of reprisal.

He swung to face the ports, avoiding the expression on the faces of the two Meloans. He'd felt something of the same on his own face when he'd first inspected Throm. But it couldn't be that bad on Meloa; she'd won her hard-earned victory!

They were entering the atmosphere now, staggering down on misfiring jets. The whole planet seemed to be covered with a gray-yellow haze that spoke of countless tons of blast dust in the air. From below, Duke heard the men beginning to move toward the big entrance lock, unable to wait for the landing. But they were no longer his responsibility. He'd given up his command before embarking.

The ship came down, threatening to tilt every second, and the pilot was sweating and swearing. The haze began to clear as they neared the ground, but the ports were too high for Duke to see anything but the underside of the thick clouds. He stood up and headed for the lift, bracing himself as the ship pitched.

Suddenly there was a sickening jar and the blast cut off. The ship groaned and seemed to twist, then was still. It was the worst landing Duke had known, but they were obviously down. A second later he heard the port screech open and the thump of the landing ramp.

The singing of the men had picked up into a rough marching beat. Now abruptly it wavered. For a moment, a few voices continued, and then died away, like a record running down. There was a mutter of voices, followed by shouts that must have been the relief officers, taking over. Duke was nearly to the port before he heard the slow, doubtful sound of steps moving down the ramp. By the time he reached it, the last of the men was just leaving. He stopped, staring at the great port city of Kordule.

Most of the port was gone. Where the hangars and repair docks had been, a crater bored into the earth, still smoking faintly. A lone girder projected above it, to mark the former great control building, and a Meloan skeleton was transfixed on it near the top. It shattered to pieces as he looked and began dropping, probably from the delayed tremor of their landing.

Even the section their ship stood on was part of the crater, he saw, with an Earth bulldozer working on it. There was room for no more than ten ships now. Two of the berths were occupied by fat Earth ships, sleek and well kept. Three others held the pitted, warped hulks of Meloan battleships. There were no native freighters, and no sign of tending equipment or hangars.

The pilot had come up behind him, following his gaze. Now the man nodded. "That's it, captain. Most cities are worse. Kordule escaped the blasts until our rocket cannon failed. Got any script on you?" At Duke's nod, he pointed. "Better exchange it at the booth, before the rate gets worse. Take Earth dollars. Our silver's no good."

He held out a hand, and Duke shook it. "Good luck, captain," he said, and swung back into the ship.

Mercifully, most of Kordule was blanketed by the dust fog. There was the beginning of a series of monstrous craters where men had begun rebuilding underground, the ruined landing field, and a section of what had been the great business district. Now it was only a field of rubble, with bits of windowless walls leading up to a crazy tangle of twisted girders. Only memory could locate where the major streets had been. Over everything lay the green wash of *incandite*, and the wind carried the smell of a charnel house. There was no sign of the apartment where he and Ronda had lived.

He started down the ramp at last, seeing for the first time the motley crew that had come out to meet the heroes of the battle of Throm. They had spotted him already, however, and some were deserting the men at the sight of his officer's uniform. Their cries mingled into an insane, whining babble in his ears.

"... Just a scrap for an old man, general ... three children at home starving ... fought under Jones, captain ... cigarette?"

It was a sea of clutching hands, ragged bodies with scrawny arms and bloated stomachs, trembling and writhing in its eagerness to get to him first. Then as one of the temporary officers swung back with a couple of field attendants, it broke apart to let him pass, its gaze riveted on him as he stumbled between the lines.

He spotted a billboard one man was wearing, and his eyes focused sharply on it. "Honest Feroiya," it announced. "Credit exchange. Best rates in all Kordule." Below that, chalked into a black square, was the important part: "2,345 credits the dollar."

Duke shook his head but the sign did not change. A quarter million credits for a hundred dollars. And he'd thought—

"Help a poor old widow." A trembling hand plucked at his sleeve, and he swung to face a woman in worse rags than the others, her eyes dull and unfocused, her lips mouthing the words only by habit. "Help the widow of General Dayole!"

He gasped as he recognized her. Five years before, he'd danced with her at a party given by Dayole—danced and agreed that the war was ruining them and that it couldn't get worse.

He reached into his pocket, before remembering the worthlessness of his bills. But there was half a pack of the wretched cigarettes issued the men. He tossed them to her and fled, while the other beggars scrambled toward her.

He walked woodenly across the leprous field, skirting away from the Earth ships, toward a collection of tents and tin huts that had swallowed the other veterans. Then he stopped and cursed to himself as a motorcycle sprang into life near the Earth freighters and came toward him. Naturally, they'd spotted his hair and skin color.

The well-fed, smooth-faced young man swung the machine beside him. "Captain O'Neill?" he asked, but his voice indicated that he was already certain. "Hop in, sir. Director Flannery has been looking forward to meeting you!"

Duke went steadily on, not varying his steps. The machine paced him uncertainly. "Director Flannery of Earth Foreign Office, Captain O'Neill. He requests your presence," he shouted over the purr of his machine. He started to swing ahead of the marching man.

Duke kept his eyes on his goal. When his steady steps almost brought him against the cycle, it roared out of his way. He could hear it behind him as he walked, but it faded.

There was only the sight and smell of Kordule ahead of him.

II

Senators were already filing through the Presidium as Edmonds of South Africa came out of his office with Daugherty of the Foreign Office. The youngest senator stopped beside the great bronze doors, studying the situation. Then he sighed in relief. "It's all right," he told Daugherty. "Premier Lesseur's presiding."

He hadn't been sure the premier's words were a full promise before. And while he hadn't been too worried, it was good to see that the doubtful vice-premier wouldn't be presiding.

"It better be all right," the diplomat said. "Otherwise, it's my neck. Cathay's counting on Earth to help against the Kloomirians, and if Director Flannery ever finds I committed us—"

Edmonds studied the seats that were filling, and nodded with more confidence as he saw that most of the senators on whom he counted were there. "I've got enough votes, as I told you. And with Lesseur presiding, the opposition won't get far with parliamentary tricks against me. This time, Earth's going to act."

Daugherty grunted, obviously still worried, and headed up the steps to the reserved Visitors' Gallery, while Edmonds moved to his seat in the assembly room. Today he didn't even mind the fact that it was back in the section reserved for the newest members—the unknowns and unimportants, from the way the press treated them. He would be neither unknown nor unimportant, once his bill was passed, and his brief experience would only add to the miracle he was working.

Looking back on his efforts, he found the results something of a miracle to himself. It had taken two years of vote-swapping, of careful propaganda, and of compromise with his principles. That business of voting for the combined Throm-Meloa Aid Bill had been a bitter thing; but old Harding was scared sick of antagonizing the aliens by seeming partiality, and Edmonds' switch was the step needed to start the softening up.

At that, he'd been lucky. In spite of what he'd learned of the manipulation of sociological relationships, in spite of the long preparation in advertising dynamics and affective psychology, he couldn't have made it if Cathay hadn't been a human colony!

Now, though, Lesseur was calling the chamber to order. The senators quieted quickly, and there was almost complete silence as the old man picked up the paper before him.

"The Senate will consider Resolution 1843 today," Lesseur said quietly. "*A Resolution that Earth shall grant assistance to the Colony of Cathay in the event of any aggressive alien act*, proposed by Sir Alfred Edmonds. Since the required time for deliberation has elapsed, the chair will admit discussion on this resolution. Senator Edmonds!"

Edmonds was on his feet, and every face turned to him. The spotlight came down on him, blinding him to the others. He picked up the microphone, polishing the words in his mind. The vote might already be decided, but the papers would still print what he said now! And those words could mean his chance to work his way up through the Committee of Foreign Affairs and perhaps on to becoming Earth's youngest premier.

It might even mean more. Once Earth shook off her lethargy and moved to her rightful position of power and strength among the humanoid worlds, anything could happen. There was the Outer Federation being formed among the frontier worlds and the nucleus of close relations with hundreds of planets. Some day there might be the position of premier of a true Interstellar Congress!

Edmonds began quietly, listening to his voice roll smoothly from the speakers, giving the long history of Earth and her rise to a position as the richest and most respected of planets. He retold the story of how she had been the first to discover the interstellar drive, and how it had inevitably spread. He touched on the envy of the alien worlds, and the friendship of the humanoid planets that had enabled Earth to found her dozen distant colonies. He couldn't wisely discuss her cowardice and timidity in avoiding her responsibilities to help her friends; but there was another approach.

"In the forefront of every battle against alien aggression," he declaimed proudly, "have been men from Earth. Millions of our young men have fought gloriously and died gladly to protect the human—and humanoid—civilizations from whatever forms of life have menaced them. Djamboula led the forces of Hera against Clovis, just as Captain O'Neill so recently directed the final battle that saved Meloa from the hordes of Throm. In our own ranks, we have a man who spent eight long and perilous years in such a gallant struggle to save a world for humanoid decency. Senator Harding—"

From the darkened sea of faces, a voice suddenly sounded. "Will the senator yield?" It was the deep baritone of Harding.

Edmonds frowned in irritation, but nodded. A few words of confirmation on his point from Harding couldn't hurt. "I yield to the senator from Dixie," he answered.

The spotlight shifted as Harding got slowly to his feet, making a white halo of his hair. He did not look at Edmonds, but turned to face Lesseur.

"Mr. Chairman," he said, "I move that Resolution 1843 be tabled!"

"Second!" The light shifted to another man, but Edmonds had no time to see who it was as he stood staring open-mouthed at Harding.

He shouted for the chair's attention, but Lesseur brought the gavel down sharply once, and his voice rang over the speakers. "It has been moved and seconded that Resolution 1843 be tabled. The senators will now vote."

Edmonds stood frozen as the voting began. Then he dropped back hastily to press the button that would turn the square bearing his number a negative red. He saw his light flash on, while other squares were lighting. When the voting was finished, there were three such red squares in a nearly solid panel of green.

"The resolution is tabled," Lesseur announced needlessly.

Harding stood up and began moving towards the rear where Edmonds sat. The junior senator was too stunned for thought. Dimly he heard something about regrets and explanations, but the words had no meaning. He felt Harding help him to his feet and begin to guide him toward the door, where someone had already brought a shocked, white-faced Daugherty.

It was then he thought of Cathay, and what his ambition and Earth's ultimate deceit and cowardice would mean to the millions there.

III

A week of the dust-filled air of Meloa had left its mark on Captain Duke O'Neill. It had spread filth over his uniform, added another year to his face, and made waking each morning a dry-throated torture. Now he stopped at the entrance to the ship where he had been reassigned a berth for the night shift. An attendant handed him a small bottle, three biscuits, and a magazine. He tasted the chemically purified water sickly, stuffed the three ersatz biscuits into his pocket, and moved down the ramp, staring at the magazine.

RONDA

It was from Earth, of course, since no printing was being done yet on Meloa. It must have come in on one of the three big Earth freighters he'd heard land during the night. Tucked into it was another of the brief notes he'd been receiving: "Director Flannery will be pleased to call on Captain O'Neill at the captain's convenience."

He shredded the note as he went across the field; he started to do the same with the news magazine, until the headlines caught his attention.

Most of the news meant nothing to him. But he skimmed the article on the eleventh planet to join the Outer Federation; the writer was obviously biased against the organization, but Duke nodded approvingly. At least someone was doing something. He saw that Cathay was in for trouble. Earth was living up to her old form! Then he shoved the magazine into his pocket and trudged on toward the veteran's reassignment headquarters.

Machinery was being moved from the Earth freighters, and Duke swore again. Five billion Earthmen would read of their "generosity" to Meloa, and any guilt they felt for their desertion would vanish in a smug satisfaction at their charity. Smugness was easy in a world without dust or carrion smell or craters that had been factories.

There were only a few Meloans in the crude tent that served as their headquarters. Duke went back toward the cubbyhole where a thin, haggard man sat on a broken block behind a makeshift desk.

The hairless blue head shook slowly while the man's eyes dropped hungrily to the paper in Duke's pocket and away again guiltily. "No work, Captain O'Neill. Unless you can operate some of those Earth machines we're getting?"

Duke grimaced, passing the magazine over to hands that trembled as they took it. His education was in ultra-literary creative writing, his experience in war. And here, where there was the whole task of rebuilding a planet to be done, the ruin of tools and power made what could be done too little for even the few who were left. There was no grain to reap or wood to cut after the killing gas from Throm had ruined vegetation; there were no workable mines where all had been blasted closed. Transportation was gone. And the economy had passed beyond hand tools, leaving too few of those. Even whole men were idle, and his artificial hand could never replace a real one for carrying rubble.

"Director Flannery has been asking for you again," the man told him.

Duke ignored it. "What about my wife?"

The Meloan frowned, reaching for a soiled scrap of paper. "We may have something. One of her former friends thinks she was near this address. We'll send someone out to investigate, if you wish, captain; but it's still pretty uncertain."

"I'll go myself," Duke said harshly. He picked up the paper, recognizing the location as one that had been in the outskirts.

The man behind the desk shook his head doubtfully. Then he shrugged, and reached behind him for a small automatic. "Better take this—and watch your step! There are two bullets left."

Duke nodded his thanks and turned away, dropping the gun into his pocket. Behind him he heard a long sigh and the rustle of a magazine being opened quickly.

It was a long walk. At first, he traced his way through streets that had been partially blasted clear. After the first mile, however, he was forced to hunt around or over the litter and wreckage, picking the way from high spot to high spot. There were people about, rooting through the debris, or patrolling in groups. He drew the automatic and carried it in his hand, in plain sight. Some stared at him and some ignored him, but none came too close.

Once he heard shouting and a group ran across his path, chasing a small rodent. He heard a wild tumult begin, minutes later. When he passed the spot where they had stopped, a fight was going on, apparently over the kill.

At noon he stopped to drink sparingly of his water and eat one of the incredibly bad biscuits. What food there was available or which could be received from the Earth freighters was being mixed into them, but it wasn't enough. The workers got a little more, and occasionally someone found a few cans under the rubble. The penalty for not turning such food in was revocation of all food allotment, but there was a small black market where unidentified cans could be bought for five Earth dollars, and some found its way there. The same black market sold the few remaining cigarettes at twice that amount each.

It was beginning to thunder to the north as he stood up and went wearily on, and the haze was thickening. He tried to hurry, uncertain of how dark it would get. If he got caught now, he'd never be able to return before night. He stumbled on a broken street sign, decoding what was left of it, and considered. Then he sighed in relief. As he remembered it, he was almost there.

The buildings had been lower here, and the rubble was thinner. There seemed to be more people about, judging by the traces of smoke that drifted out of holes or through glassless windows. He saw none outside, however.

He was considering trying one of the places from which smoke was coming when he saw the little boy five hundred feet ahead. He started forward, but the kid popped into what must have been a cellar once. Duke stopped, calling quietly.

This time it was a girl of about sixteen who appeared. She sidled closer, her eyes fixed on his hair. Her voice piped out suddenly, scared and desperate. "You lonesome, Earthman?" Under the fright, it was a grotesque attempt at coquetry. She edged nearer, staring at him. "I won't roll you, honest!"

"All I want is information," he told her thickly. "I'm looking for a woman named Ronda—Ronda O'Neill. She was my wife."

The girl considered, shaking her head. Her eyes grew wider as he pulled out a green Earth bill, but she didn't move. Then, as he added the two remaining biscuits, she nodded quickly, motioning him forward. "Mom might know," she said.

She ran ahead, and soon an older woman shuffled up the broken steps. In her arms was a baby, dead or in a coma, and she rocked it slowly, moaning softly as she listened to his questions. She grunted finally, and reached out for the reward. Shuffling ahead of him, she went up the rubble-littered street and around a corner, to point. "Go in," she said. "Ronda'll be back."

Duke shoved the crude door back and stepped into what was left of a foyer in a cheap apartment house. The back had been blasted away, but the falling building had sealed over one corner, covering it from most of the weather. Light came from the shattered window, showing a scrap of blanket laid out on the floor near a few possessions. At first, nothing identified the resident in any way, and he wondered if it were a trap. Then he bent over a broken bracelet, and his breath caught sharply. The catch still worked, and a faded miniature of him was inside the little holder. Ronda's!

Duke dropped onto the blanket, trying to imagine what Ronda would be like, and to picture the reunion. But the present circumstances wouldn't fit into anything he could imagine. He could only remember the bravely smiling girl who had seen him off five years before.

He heard a babble of voices outside, but he didn't look out. The walk had exhausted him. Hard as the bed was, it was better than standing up. Anyhow, if Ronda came back, he was pretty sure she would be warned of his presence.

He slept fitfully, awakened by the smells and sounds from outside. Once he thought someone looked in, but he couldn't be sure. He turned over, almost decided to investigate, and dozed off again.

It was the hoarse sound of breathing and a soft shuffle that wakened him that time. His senses jarred out of slumber with a feeling of wrongness that reacted in instant caution. He let his eyes slit open, relieved to find there was still light.

Between him and the door, a figure was creeping up on hands and knees. The rags of clothes indicated it was a woman and the knife in one hand spelled murder!

Duke snapped himself upright to a sitting position, his hand darting for the gun in his pocket. A low shriek came from the woman, and she lunged forward, the knife rising. There was no time for the gun. He caught her wrist, twisting savagely. She scratched and writhed, but the knife spun from her grasp. With a moan, she collapsed across his knees.

He turned her face up, staring at it unbelievingly. "Ronda!"

Bloated and stained, lined with fear, it still bore a faint resemblance to the girl he had known. Now a fleeting look of cunning crossed her face briefly, to be replaced with an attempt at dawning recognition. "Duke!" She gasped it, then made a sound that might have been meant for joy. She stumbled to her knees, reaching out to him. But her eyes swiveled briefly toward the knife. "Duke, it's you!"

He pushed her back and reached for the knife. He was sure she'd known who it was—had probably been the one who awakened him by looking in through the broken window. "Why'd you try to kill me, Ronda? You saw who it was. If you needed money, you know I'd give you anything I had. Why?"

"Not for money." She twisted from him and slumped limply against a broken wall. Tears came into her eyes. This time the catch in her voice was real. "I know ... I know, Duke. And I wanted to see you, to talk to you, too." She shook her head slowly. "What can I do with money? I wanted to wake you up like old times. But Mrs. Kalaufa—she led you here—she said—"

He waited, but she didn't finish. She traced a pattern on the dust of the floor, before looking up again. "You've never been really hungry! Not that hungry! You wouldn't understand."

"Even with the dole, you can't starve that much in the time since Kordule was bombed," he protested. He gagged as he thought of the meaning he'd guessed from her words, expecting her to deny it.

She shrugged. "In ten years, you can do anything. Oh, sure, you came back on leave and we lived high. Everything was fine here, wasn't it? Sure it was, for you. They briefed me on where I should take you, so there'd be good food ready. They kept a few places going for the men who came back on leave. We couldn't ruin your morale!"

She laughed weakly, and let the sound die away slowly. "How do you think we sent out the food and supplies for the fleet the last three years, after the blockade on our supplies from friendly worlds? Why do you think there was no more leave for you? Because they didn't think you brave soldiers could stand just seeing how the rest of us lived! And you think you had it tough! Watch the sky for the enemy while your stomach hopes for the sound that might be a rat. Hide three cans of food you'll be shot for hoarding—because there is nothing else important in the world. And then have a man steal them from you when the raids come! What does a soldier know of war?"

The sickness inside him grew into a knot, but he still couldn't fully believe what she was saying. "But cannibalism—"

"No." She shook her head with a faint trace of his own disgust. "No, Duke. Mrs. Kalaufa told me ... you're not really the same race—Not as close as you are to an Earth animal, and you don't call that cannibalism. Nobody on Meloa has ever been a cannibal—yet! How much money do you have, Duke?"

He took it out and handed it to her. She counted it mechanically and handed it back. "Not enough. You can't take me away when you leave here."

"I'm not leaving," he told her. He dropped the money back on the blanket beside her.

She stared at him for a moment and then pulled herself up to her feet, moving toward the door. "Good-by, Duke. And get off Meloa. You can't help us any more. And I don't want you here when I get desperate enough to remember you might take me back. I like you too much for that, even now."

He took a step toward her, and she ducked.

"Get out!" She screamed it at him. "Do you think I can stand looking at you without drooling any longer? Do you want me to call Mrs. Kalaufa for help?"

Through the open door, he saw Mrs. Kalaufa across the street, still cradling the child. As the door slammed shut behind him, the woman screamed, either as a summons or from fear that he'd seek revenge on her. He saw other heads appear, with frantic eyes that stared sullenly at the gun he carried. He stumbled down the street, where rain was beginning to fall, conscious that it would be night before he got back to the port. He no longer cared.

There was no place for him here, he now saw. He was still an Earthman, and Earthmen were always treated as a race apart somehow. He didn't belong. Nor could he go back to a life on Earth. But there were still the recruiting stations there; so long as war existed, there had to be such stations. He headed for the fat ships of Earth that squatted complacently on the wrecked port.

IV

Prince Queeth of Sugfarth had left the royal belt behind, and only a plain band encircled his round little body as he trotted along, his four legs making almost no sound. His double pair of thin arms and the bird-like head on his long neck bobbed excitedly in time to his steps. Once he stopped to glance across the black stone buildings of the city as they shone in the dull red of the sun, toward the hill where his father's palace was lighted brightly for the benefit of his Earth guests. Queeth touched his ears together ceremoniously and then trotted on, until he came to the back door of his group's gymnasium. He whistled the code word and the door opened automatically.

The whole group was assembled, though it was past sleep week for most of them. Their ears clicked together, but they waited silently as he curled himself up in the official box. Then Krhal, the merchant viscount, whistled questioningly. "This will have to be important, Queeth."

The prince bobbed his ears emphatically. "It is. My father's guests have all the news, and I learned everything. It won't be as long as we thought." He paused, before delivering the big news. "The bipeds of Kloomiria are going to attack Cathay. There'll be official war there within two weeks!"

He saw them exchanging hasty signals, but again it was Krhal who voiced their question. "And you think that is important, Queeth? What does it offer us? Cathay is a human colony. Earth will have to declare war with her. And with Earth's wealth, it will be over before we could arrive."

"Earth has already passed a resolution that neutrality will apply to colonies as well as to other planets!"

This time the whistles were sharper. Krhal had difficulty believing it at first. "So Earth really is afraid to fight? That must mean those rumors that she has no fleet are true. Our ancestors thought so, and even planned to attack her, before the humanoids defeated us. The ancestor king believed that even a single ship fully armed might conquer her."

"It could be," Queeth admitted. "But do you agree that this is the news for which we've waited so long?"

There was a quick flutter of cars. "It's our duty," Krhal agreed. "In a war between Cathay and Kloomiria, we can't remain neutral if we're ever to serve our friends. Well, the ship is ready!"

That came as a surprise to Queeth. He knew the plans were well along, but not that they were completed. As merchant viscount, and second-degree adult, Krhal was entitled to a tenth of his father's interests. He'd chosen the biggest freighter and the balance in fluid assets, to the pleasure of his father— who believed he was planning an honorable career of exploring.

"The conversion completed?" Queeth asked. "But the planet bombs—!"

"Earth supplied them on the last shipment. I explained on the order that I was going to search uninhabited planets for minerals."

Queeth counted the group again, and was satisfied. There were enough. With a ship of that size, fully staffed and armed, they would be a welcome addition to any fleet. They might be enough to tip the balance for victory, in fact. And while Cathay and Kloomiria lay a long way on the other side of Earth's system, the drives were fast enough to cover it in two weeks.

"Does your father know?" Krhal asked.

Queeth smirked. "Would you tell him? He still believes along with the Earth ambassador that the warrior strain was ruined among our people when we lost the war with the humanoids."

"Maybe it was," Krhal said doubtfully. "In four generations, it could evolve again. And there are the books and traditions from which we trained. If even a timid race such as those of Earth can produce warriors like O'Neill—a mere poet—why can't the Sugfarth do better? Particularly when Earth rebuilt factories for us to start our shipbuilding anew."

"Then we join the war," the prince decided.

There was a series of assent signals from the group.

"Tonight," he suggested, and again there was only assent.

Krhal stood up, setting the course for the others. When the last had risen, Queeth uncurled himself and rose from the box. "We'll have to pass near Earth," he suggested as they filed out toward the hangars where Krhal kept his ship. "Maybe we should show our intentions there!"

There was a sudden whistle of surprise. Then the assent was mounting wildly. Queeth trotted ahead toward the warship, making his attack plans over again as he realized he was a born leader who could command such enthusiasm. He had been doubtful before, in spite of his study of elementary statistical treatment of relationships.

The lights in the palace showed that the Earth guests were still celebrating as the great, heavily-laden warship blasted up and headed toward Earth.

V

Duke O'Neill found a corner of the lounge where no Earthman was near and dropped down with the magazine and papers, trying to catch up on the currents of the universe as they affected the six hundred connected worlds. Most of the articles related to Earth alone, and he skipped them. He found one on the set-up of the Outer Federation finally. The humanoid planets there were in a pocket of alien worlds, and union had been almost automatic. It was still loose, but it seemed to have sound enough a basis.

If Earth had been willing to come out of its shell and risk some of its fat trading profits, there could have been an even stronger union that would have driven war-like thoughts out of the minds of all the aliens.

Instead, she seemed to be equally interested in building up her potential enemies and ruining her friends. Duke had watched a showing of new films on the work being done on Throm the night before, and he was still sick from it. Throm had lost the war, but by a military defeat, not by thirty-one unprotected raids on all her surface. She still had landing fields equipped for Earth ships, and the big freighters were dropping down regularly, spewing out foods, equipment and even heavy machinery for her rebuilding. Throm was already on the road back. Meloa had to wait until she could pull herself up enough to build fields.

Duke turned his eyes to the port. The ship had stopped at Clovis on the way back to Earth. From where he sat, he could see almost Earth-like skyscrapers stretching up in a great city. The landing field was huge, and there were rows on rows of factories building more of the freighters that stubbed the field.

It seemed impossible, when he remembered that only forty years had passed since Djamboula's suicide raid had finally defeated the fungoid creatures of the planet and since the survivors' vows to repay all Earthmen for their defeat. They were a prolific race, of course—but without help from Earth, the factories would be shacks and the rockets and high-drive ships would be only memories.

He wondered how many were cursing their ancestors for making the mistake of attacking a neighboring humanoid planet instead of Earth, only two days away on high drive. By now, they knew that Earth was defenseless. And yet, they seemed content to go on with their vows forgotten. Duke couldn't believe it. Down underground, beyond Earth inspection, they could have vast stockpiles of weapons, ready to install in their ships within days.

How could Earth risk it, unless she had her own stock of hidden ships and weapons? Yet if she did, he was sure that it would have been impossible not to use them in defense of the colony of Cathay.

He stared out, watching the crewmen mixing with the repulsive alien natives, laughing as they worked side by side. There must be some factor he didn't understand, but he'd never found it—nor did he know anyone who had guessed it.

He stirred, uncomfortable with his own thoughts. But it wasn't fear for Earth that bothered him. It was simply that sooner or later some alien race would risk whatever unknown power the others feared. If the aliens won, the vast potential power of Earth would then be turned against all the humanoid races of the universe. Humanity could be driven from the galaxy.

He turned the pages, idly glancing at the headlines. It was hard to realize that the paper wasn't right off the presses of Earth; it must have been brought out to Clovis on the latest ship. He checked the date, and frowned in surprise. According to the rough calendar he'd kept, it was the current date. Somewhere he must have lost track of two days. How much else had he lost sight of during the long years of war?

A diagram caught his attention almost at once as he turned to another magazine. It was of a behemoth ship, bigger than any he had ever seen, and built like the dream of a battleship, though it was listed as a freighter. He scanned it, mentally converting it. With a few like that, Meloa could have won during the first year.

Then he swore as he saw it was part of an article on the progress of some alien world known as Sugfarth—by the article, a world of former warriors, once dedicated to the complete elimination of humanoids!

He saw Flannery coming along the deck at that moment, and he picked up the magazine, heading for his cabin. He'd ignored previous summons on the thin excuse of not feeling well. He had no desire to talk with Earthmen. It was bad enough to take their charity back to Earth and to have to stay on the planet until he could sign on with the Outer Federation. His memories were ugly enough, without having them refreshed.

But Flannery caught him as he was opening the door to his cabin. The director was huge, with heavy, strong features and a body that looked too robust for the white hair and the age that showed around his eyes. His voice was tired, however, showing his years more plainly than his looks.

"Captain O'Neill," he said quickly. "Stop jousting with windmills. It's time you grew up. Besides, I've got a job for you."

"Does my charity passage demand an interview, director?" Duke asked.

The other showed no offense, unfortunately. He smiled wryly. "If I choose, it does. I'm in command of this ship, as well as head of the Foreign Office. May I come in?"

"I can't keep you out," Duke admitted. He dropped onto the couch, sprawling out, while the other found the single chair.

Flannery picked up the magazine and glanced through it. "So you're interested in the Outer Federation?" he asked. "Don't be. It doesn't have a chance. In a week or so, you'll see it shot. And I don't mean we'll wreck it. They've picked their own doom, against all the advice we could give them. Care to have a drink sent down while we talk?"

Duke shook his head. "I'd rather cut it short."

"Hotheads," Flannery told the walls thoughtfully, "make the best men obtainable, once they're tamed. Nothing beats an idealist who can face facts. And the intelligent ones usually grow up. Captain, I've studied your strategy against Throm on that last drive after Dayole was killed. Brilliant! I need a good man, and I can pay for one. If you give me a chance, I can also show you why you should take it. Know anything about how Earth got started on its present course?"

"Dumb luck and cowardice, as far as I can see," Duke answered.

When Earth discovered the first inefficient version of the high drive, she had found herself in a deserted section of the universe, with the nearest inhabited star system months away. The secret of the drive couldn't be kept, of course, but the races who used it to build war fleets found it easier to fight with each other than with distant Earth. Later, when faster drives were developed, Earth was protected by the buffer worlds she had rebuilt.

Flannery grinned. "Luck—and experience. We learned something from our early nuclear-technological wars. We learned more from the interstellar wars of others. We decided that any planet ruined by such war wouldn't fight again—the women and children who lived through that hell would see to it—unless new hatreds grew up during the struggle back. So we practically pauperized ourselves at first to see that they recovered too quickly for hate and fear. We also began digging into the science of how to manipulate relationships—Earth's greatest discovery—to set up a system that would work. It paid off for us in the long run."

"So what's all that got to do with me?" Duke asked. He'd heard of the great science of Earth and her ability to manipulate all kinds of relationships before, spoken of in hush-hush terms when he was still in college. But he'd quit believing in fairy tales even before then. Now he was even sicker of Earth's self-justification.

Flannery frowned, and then shrugged. "It's no secret I need a good man on Throm, and you're the logical candidate, if I can pound some facts into your head. I've found that sending an Earthman they know as a competent enemy works wonders. Not at first—there's hostility for a while—but in the long run it gives them a new slant on us."

"Then you'd better get an Earthman," Duke snapped. "You're talking to a citizen of Meloa! By choice!"

"I hadn't finished my explanation," Flannery reminded.

Duke snorted. "I was brought up on explanations. I heard men spouting about taming the aliens when I first learned to talk—as if they were wild animals. I read articles on how the Clovisem and those things from Sugfarth needed kindness. It's the same guff I heard about how to handle lions. But the men doing the talking weren't in the ring; and I noticed the ringmaster carried a whip and gun. He knew the beasts. I know the aliens of Throm."

"From fighting them? From hating them? Or from being more afraid of them than you think Earth is, captain? I've talked to more aliens than you've ever seen."

"And the Roman diplomats laughed at the soldiers who told them the Goths were getting ready to sack Rome."

Flannery stared at him in sudden amusement. "We aren't in an Empire period, O'Neill. But you might look up what the Romans did to conquered people during the Republic, when Rome was still growing. Captain, I'm not underrating the aliens!"

"Tame aliens! Or ones faking tameness. You've seen them smiling, maybe. I saw the other side."

The old man sighed heavily and reached for his shirt. He began unbuttoning it and pulling it over his head. "You've got a nice prosthetic hand," he said. "Now take a look at some real handiwork!"

There was a strap affair around his shoulders, with a set of complicated electronic controls slipped into the muscle fibers. From them, both arms hung loose, unattached at the shoulder blades. Further down, another affair of webbing went around his waist.

"Only one leg is false," he explained, "but the decorations are real. They came from a highly skilled torturer. I've had my experience with aliens. Clovisem, if you're curious. I was the second in command on Djamboula's volunteer raid, forty years ago."

Duke dropped his eyes from the scars. For a second, he groped for words of apology. Then the cold, frozen section of his brain swallowed the emotions. "I've seen a woman with a prosthetic soul," he said bitterly. "Only she didn't turn yellow because of what the aliens did!"

Red spots shot onto Flannery's cheeks and one of the artificial arms jerked back as savagely as a real one. He hesitated, then reached for his shirt. "O.K., squawman!"

The word had no meaning for Duke, though he knew it was an insult. But he couldn't respond to it. He fumbled through his memories, trying to place it. Something about Indians—

Flannery began buttoning his pants over the shirt. "I'm out of bounds, captain," he said more quietly. "I hope you don't know the prejudices behind that crack. But you win. If you ever want the rest of the explanation, look me up."

He closed the door behind him softly and went striding evenly up the passage.

Duke frowned after him. The talk had gotten under his skin. If there were things he didn't know—

Then he swore at himself. There was plenty he didn't know. But the carefully developed indoctrination propaganda of the top Earth psychologists wasn't the answer he wanted.

He'd have to make his stay on Earth shorter than he'd planned. If they could get to a man who had served under Djamboula and convince him that Clovisem were nice house pets, it was little wonder they could wrap the rest of Earth around their psychological fingers.

Too bad their psychology wasn't adjusted to aliens!

VI

Barth Nevesh was nearly seven feet tall, and his cat-shaped ears stuck up another four inches above his head. Even among the people of Kel he was a big man, but to the representatives of the other humanoid worlds of the Federation, he seemed a giant. The thick furs he wore against the heavy chill of the room added to his apparent size, and the horns growing from his shoulders lifted his robes until he seemed to have no neck.

Now he stood up, driving his heavy fist down against the big wooden table. "The question is, do we have the answer or not?" he roared. "You say we do. Logic says we do. Then let's act on it!"

The elfin figure of Lemillulot straightened up at the other end of the table. "Not so fast, commander. Nobody questions the power of your fleet. Nobody doubts that we have the only possible answer to the aliens that Earth is helping to take over our universe—strength through unity. But is it as good as it can be?"

"How better?" Barth roared again. "Every world in this alien pocket has been building its strength since the Earthmen's ships first reached here and showed us space travel was possible. We've seen the stinking aliens get the same ships. But now we've got something they can't resist—a Federation, in spite of all Earth could do to stop us. If all our fleets strike at once, no alien world can resist—and we can stop merely holding them back. Wipe them out, one by one, I say! The only good alien is a dead alien!"

There was a lot of talk—more than Barth usually heard or contributed in a month. Lemillulot was the focus of most of it. The little man would never be satisfied. He wanted all the humanoid worlds organized, and by now it was plain that Earth's influence would be too strong outside of their own section.

Their accomplishments were already enough. United as they were, the Federation was clearly invincible. Their fleets were at full size and the crews were thoroughly trained. No other time would be better.

There had already been a stir of ship-building on the alien worlds, since the first word of the Federation had somehow leaked out. The Federation position was as good as it would ever be—and with eleven fleets working together, nothing better was needed.

"Knock them down with the long shells, haze them to base with interceptors, and then rip their worlds with planet bombs," Barth repeated his plans. "We can do it in six hours for a planet—we can start at the strongest, Neflis, and work down through the weakest, to make up for our losses. And if the Earth forces start moving in to rebuild them—well, I've been thinking the Federation could use a little more wealth and power!"

"Humanoids don't attack humanoids," Lemillulot protested.

The snarling, dog face of Sra from Chumkt opened in a grin, and his sly voice held a hint of a chuckle. "Or so Earth keeps preaching. But Earthmen aren't humanoids. They're humans!"

He laughed softly at his own wit. There were rumbles of uncertainty, but Barth saw that the seed had taken root. If they kept working together, he and Sra could force it to ripen soon enough.

"That can wait," Barth decided. "The question is, do we attack Neflis, and when? I say now!"

It took an hour more for the decision. But there would be only one answer, and the final vote was unanimous. The fleets would take off from their home worlds and rendezvous near the barren sun; from there, they would proceed in a group, under the control of Barth, toward the alien world of Neflis.

The commander checked his chronometer as the delegates went to send their coded reports to their home worlds. He had the longest distance to lead his fleet, and there was no time for delay.

Outside, the harsh snow crackled under his feet, and a layer of storm clouds cut off the wan heat of Kel's sun. He drew in a deep breath, watching the swirl of white as he exhaled. It was a good world—a world to build men. It was the world from which a leader should come.

The fleet would be all his within a day. And for a time, it would be busy at the work of wiping out the nearby aliens. After that—well, there were other aliens further out toward the last frontiers of exploration. With care, the fleet could be kept busy for years.

Barth was remembering his histories, and the armies that had been swept together. In a few years, fighting men began to think of themselves as a people apart, and loyalty to their birthplace gave way to loyalty to their leader. Five years should be enough. Then there could be more than a Federation; there could be the empire among the worlds that had been his lifelong dream.

But first, there was Earth. He snorted to himself as he reached the ships of his fleet. Missionaries! Spreading their soft fear through the universe. In five years, his fleet should be ready for ten times the power of any single planet— including Earth.

Sra would be the only problem in his way. But that could be met later. For the moment, the man from Chumkt was useful.

Barth strode up the ramp of his flagship, shouting out to his men as he went. There was no need of signals. They had been primed and waiting for days, ready to follow him up.

He dropped to the control seat, staring at the little lights that would tell him of their progress. "Up ship!" he shouted, and from the metal halls and caverns of the ship other voices echoed his cry.

The *Wind Dragon* leaped upwards sharply. Behind, as the red lights showed, four hundred others charged into the sky and the open space beyond. Barth sat at the great screen, watching as they drew on steadily toward the rendezvous, mulling over his plans.

They were three hours out from Kel when he turned the control over to his lieutenant and went below, where his table was laden with the smoking cheer of good green meat and ale. With a sigh of contentment, he threw back his outer robe and prepared to forget everything until he had dined.

He was humming hoarsely to himself as he cut a piece of the meat and stuck it on his left shoulder horn, within reach of his teeth. Maybe a little of the baked fish would blend well—

The emergency drum blasted through the ship as he lifted the knife. Swearing and tearing at the flesh near his mouth, he leaped up and forward toward the control room. He heard voices shouting, something about a fleet. Then he was at the screens where he could see for himself.

Five million miles ahead, another fleet was assembled, where none should be from any of the Federation worlds! His eyes swept sideways across the screen, estimating the number. It was impossible. There weren't a quarter of that number in the fleet of any world, humanoid or alien!

Barth flipped on the microresolver, twisting the wheel that sent it racing across the path of the fleet ahead. His eyes confirmed what his mind had already recognized.

The aliens had their own federation. There were ships of every type there, grouped in units. Thirteen alien worlds were combined against the Outer Federation.

For a breath he hesitated, ready to turn back and defend Kel while there was time. But it would never work. One fleet would never be enough to defend the planet against the combined aliens.

"Cluster!" he barked into the communicator. "Out rams and up speed. Prepare for breakthrough!"

If they could hit the aliens at full drive and cut through the weaker center, they could still rendezvous with the other fleets. The combined strength might be enough. And the gods help Kel if the aliens refused to follow him!

Earth, he thought; Earth again, coddling and protecting aliens, forming them into a conspiracy against the humanoid worlds. If Kel or any part of the Federation survived, that debt would be paid!

VII

Earth lay fat and smug under the sun, seemingly unchanged since Duke had left it. For generations the populace had complained that they were draining themselves dry to rebuild other worlds, but they had grown rich on the investment. It was the only planet where men worked shorter and shorter hours to give them more leisure in which to continue a frantic effort to escape boredom. It was also the only world where the mention of aliens made men think of their order books instead of their weapons.

Duke walked steadily away from the grotesquely elaborate landing field. He had less than thirty cents in his pocket, but his breakfast aboard had left him satisfied for the moment. He turned onto a wider street, heading the long distance across the city toward the most probable location of the recruiting stations.

The Outer Federation station would be off the main section, since the official line was disapproving of such a union. But he was sure there would be one. The system of recruiting was a tradition too hard to break. Earth used it as an escape valve for her troublemakers. And since such volunteers made some of the best of all fighters, they had already decided the outcome of more than one war. By carefully juggling the attention given the stations, Earth could influence the battles without seeming to do so.

The air was thick with the smell of late summer, and there was pleasure in that, until Duke remembered the odor of Meloa, and its cause. Later the cloying perfume of women mixed with the normal industrial odors of the city, until his nose was overdriven to the point of cutoff. He saw things in the shop windows that he had forgotten, but he had no desire for them. And over everything came the incessant yammer of voices saying nothing, radios blaring, television babbling, and vending machines shouting.

He gave up at last and invested half his small fund in a subway. It was equally noisy, but it took less time. Beside him, a fungoid creature from Clovis was busy practicing silently on its speaking machine, but nobody else seeemed to notice.

Duke's head was spinning when he reached the surface again. He stopped to let it clear, wondering if he'd ever found this world home. It wouldn't matter soon, though; once he was signed up at the recruiting station, there would be no time to think.

He saw the sign, only a few blocks from where the recruiting posters for Meloa had been so long ago. It was faded, but he could read the lettering, and he headed for it. As he had expected, it was on a dirty back street, where the buildings were a confusion of shipping concerns and cheaper apartment houses.

He knew something was wrong when he was a block away. There was no pitch being delivered by a barking machine, and no idle group watching the recruiting efforts on the street. In fact, nobody was in front of the vacant store that had been used, and the big posters were ripped down.

He reached the entrance and stopped. The door was half open, but it carried a notice that the place had been closed by order of the World Foreign Office. Through the dirty glass, Duke could see a young man of about twenty sitting slumped behind a battered desk.

He stepped in and the boy looked up apathetically. "You're too late, captain. Neutrality went on hours ago when the first word came through. Caught me just ready to ship out—after two lousy months recruiting here, I have to be the one stranded."

"You're lucky," Duke told him mechanically, not sure whether he meant it or not. Oddly, the idea of a kid like this mixed up in an interplanetary war bothered him. He turned to go, then hesitated. "Got a newspaper or a directory around that I could borrow?"

The boy fished a paper out of a wastebasket. "It's all yours, captain. The whole place is yours. Slam the door when you go out. I'm going over to the Cathay office."

"I'll go along," Duke offered. The address of that place was all he'd wanted from the paper. He'd have preferred the Federation to joining up with Earth colonists, but beggars never made good choosers.

The kid shook his head. He dragged open a drawer, found a slip of paper, and handed it over. It was a notice that the legal maximum age for recruiting had been reduced to thirty! "You'd never make it, captain," he said.

Duke looked at the paper in his hands and at the dim reflection of his face in a window. "No," he agreed. "I didn't make it."

He followed the boy to the door, staring out at the street, thick with its noises and smells. He dropped to the doorsill and looked briefly up at the sky where two ships were cutting out to space. Flannery had known the regulation and hadn't told him. Yet it was his own fault; the age limit was lower now, but there had always been a limit. He had simply forgotten that he'd grown older.

He found it hard to realize he'd been no older than the kid when he'd signed up for the war with Throm.

For a while he sat looking at the street, trying to realize what had happened to him. It took time to face the facts. He listened with half his attention as a small group of teen-age boys came from one of the buildings and began exchanging angry insults with another group apparently waiting for them on the corner. From their attitudes, some of them were carrying weapons and were half-eager, half-afraid to use them. It was hard to remember back to the time when such things had seemed important to him. He considered putting a stop to the argument, before it got out of hand, since no police were near; but adults had no business in kid fights. He watched them retreat slowly back to an alley, still shouting to work up their courage. Maybe he should be glad that there was even this much fire left under the smug placidity of Earth.

Finally, he picked up the newspaper from where he'd dropped it and began turning back to the want ads. His needs were few, and there should be dishwashing jobs, at least, somewhere in the city. He still had to eat and find some place to sleep.

A headline glared up at him, catching his attention. He started to skim the story, and then read it thoroughly. Things weren't going at all as he'd expected in the Outer Worlds, if the account were true; and usually, such battle reports weren't altered much.

The aliens had developed a union of their own—if anything, a stronger one than the humanoids had. Apparently they'd chased the Federation ships into some kind of a trap. Losses on both sides were huge. And raids had begun on all the alien and humanoid planets.

He scowled as he came to the latest developments. One section of the Federation fleet under Sra of Chumkt had pulled out, accusing the faction headed by Barth Nevesh of leading the aliens to the humanoid rendezvous. Kel's leader had gone after the deserters, fought it out with them in the middle of the larger battle, killed Sra, and declared himself the head of the whole Federation. It was madness that should have led to complete annihilation; only the fumbling, uncoördinated leadership of the aliens had saved the humanoid fleets. And now the Federation was coming apart at the seams, with Barth Nevesh frantically scurrying around to catch up the pieces.

Duke read it through again, but with no added information. It was a shock to know that the aliens had combined against the humanoid Federation. Still, looking back on that, he could begin to see that they would have to, once they knew of the Federation. But the rest of the account—

Flannery's words came back to him. The director had been right. His prediction was already coming true, after only three days—unless he had either had prior knowledge or juggled things to make it come true! Duke considered it, but he could see no way Flannery could either learn or act in advance of the arrival of the ship on Earth. The Federation was farther from Meloa than from this planet. He'd been forced to depend on the same accounts Duke had read in the papers on board the ship.

Then Duke glanced at the date on the current paper idly, and his thoughts jolted completely out of focus. It was dated only three days later than the paper he had seen when they were docked on Clovis! Without instantaneous communication, it was impossible. He might have been mistaken about the date before, but—

Nothing fitted. The feeling of uncertainty came back, crowding out the minor matter of his memory of the date. He stared at the richness of even this poor section of an Earth that huddled here as if afraid of its own shadows, yet reeked with self-satisfaction. He thought of Meloa and Throm, and the gallant try at Federation that had been made on the Outer Worlds. Strength had to lie in union and action; yet all the evidence seemed to say that it lay in timidity and sloth.

Reluctantly he turned the page away from the news, to seek for the job sections. From the alley, there came the sound of a police whistle, and shouts that faded into the distance. It was probably the breaking up of the teen-age argument. A few people ran by, heading for the excitement, but Duke had lost all interest. A taxi stopped nearby and he heard a patter that might have been that of children's feet, but he didn't look up.

Then a sharper whistle shrilled almost in his ear and he twisted around to stare at a creature who was gazing at him. Four spindly legs led up to a globular body encased in a harness-like contraption. Above the body, two pairs of thin arms were waving about, while a long neck ended in a bird-like head, topped by two large ears.

The ears suddenly seemed to shimmer in the air, and a surprisingly human voice sounded. "You're Captain Duke O'Neill!"

Before Duke could answer, a small hand came out quickly to find his and begin shaking it, while the ears twittered on in excitement. "I'm honored to meet you, Captain O'Neill. I've been studying your work against Throm. Amazingly clever strategy! Permit me—I'm Queeth, lately a prince of Sugfarth. Perhaps you noticed our ship? No, of course not. You must have landed at the government field. My crew and I are on the way to the war about to begin between Kloomiria and Cathay."

"Why tell me about it?" Duke asked roughly. Sugfarth—the ship he'd seen diagrammed had come from there. If one of those titans was to be used against Cathay, Earth's colony was doomed. And the impertinent little monster—!

The creature tried to imitate a shrug with his upper set of arms. "Why not, captain? We're registered here as a recruiting ship for Cathay, so it's no secret. We thought we might as well carry along some of the men going out to help, since we had to pass near Earth anyhow. And I dropped by here in the hope that there might be a few who had failed to join the Federation and who would like to switch to Cathay."

"Wait a minute," Duke said. He studied the alien, trying to rake what he'd learned from the article out of his memory. But no record of subtlety or deceit had been listed there. The Sugfarth were supposed to be honest—in fact, they'd been one of the rare races to declare their war in advance. Somehow, too, the words had a ring of truth in them. "*For* Cathay?"

"Certainly, captain. For whom else? The civilized Earth races naturally have to stick together against the barbarians."

Duke stared at the almost comic figure, juggling the words he had heard with the obvious facts. "What Earth races? Do you mean that Earth is now giving citizenship to your people?"

"Not on this planet, of course." A pair of beady black eyes stared back, as if trying to understand a ridiculous question. "But we're citizens of Earth's economic-cultural-diplomatic system, naturally."

Duke felt something nibble at his mind, but he couldn't grasp it. And he wasn't accustomed to carrying on long chitchat with aliens. He shoved the thoughts away and reached for the paper again. "You won't find recruits here, Queeth. Only me. And I'm too old for the recruiting law. Besides, I've got to find a job."

He turned the pages, locating the column he wanted. What had Flannery meant about Republican Rome? Duke could remember dimly something about Rome's granting citizenship to her conquered neighbors. It had been the basis of the city's growth and later power. Now if Earth could inspire citizenship from conquered aliens—

Queeth made a sound like a sigh and shuffled his four feet on the sidewalk uncertainly. "If you came aboard on a visit, who could stop our taking off at

"Up, surround them, blast them!" he ordered. A few might get through to the ships or to the planet below, but quick action would wreak havoc among them and discourage further attempts.

The Kloomirian fleet opened into a circle and began rising. Now the swarm of little ships began breaking apart, fanning out and attempting to turn. Var hissed. Not even the courage to go through with it after they were discovered! They—

He leaped to the screen, cursing at what he saw.

Where the little ships had opened a hole, a monstrous bulk was hurtling through at fantastic speed. The tiny ships had screened it, but now it outran them, boring straight toward the opening in the Kloomirian fleet. Atomic cannon began running out of enormous hatches, like the bristles jutting from a tendril brush.

"Blast out!" Var screamed into his engine phone. His flagship leaped away at full drive, while the enemy seemed to grow on the screen. Then it diminished as they began drawing away from the fleet.

There was nothing Var could do about the horror that followed. The great vessel bored through the fleet with cannons spitting out hell. If countershots were fired, they had no effect.

"Sugfarth!" the aide screamed in his ears. "A ship from Sugfarth!"

Var remembered the pictures he had seen, and they matched, though none had suggested such a size. It was impossible. The race of Sugfarth were aliens—warriors who had fought humanoids as few races had done. They would have fought with him, not against him!

The ship drove down toward the planet, braking fiercely now. From it, two bulky objects fell. While the planet bombs dropped, the behemoth began to rise again. It came through the shattered ranks of Kloomiria's fleet, blasting again, and headed toward the tiny ships that had screened it, new hatches opening to receive them.

Half of Var's fleet was in total ruin. On the planet below, two horrible gouts of flame leaped up through the atmosphere and beyond it, while all of Kloomiria seemed to tremble as half a continent was ruined. Var stared down at the destruction, unmoving.

The aide coughed, holding out another roll of paper. "Cathay is broadcasting an appeal for us to surrender without reprisals, magnificence. And the Estate Governors are demanding fleet protection."

Var crushed the paper in his hands without reading it.

It would take half the remaining part of the fleet to give even token protection to Kloomiria. His plans had never been based on holding back the seemingly weak forces of Cathay.

"No answer," he said. His hand reached for the communicator switch and he began issuing orders. "The fleet will regroup and return to base for immediate repairs and rearming. Commanders of *all* ships will prepare to take off against Cathay within six hours!"

Somehow, the humans had to be crushed completely before they could destroy Kloomiria. After that, if any of his race survived, there would be a mission for all future generations.

Only the power of Earth could have sent the alien ship from Sugfarth, loaded with cannon and bombs, to fight against fellow aliens. Earth had declared neutrality, and then struck! For such a villainy, a million years was not too long to seek vengeance!

IX

Night had fallen in the park beyond the huge Foreign Office building and the air was damp and cool. Duke shivered in the shadows that covered his bench. He should head back to his room, but he had no desire to listen again to the meaningless chatter that came through the thin walls. Time didn't matter to him now, anyhow.

He swore and reached for a cigarette, brushing the crumpled newspaper from his lap. He'd been a fool to think Flannery would bother with him, just as he'd been a fool to turn down Queeth's offer. He'd wasted his day off from the messenger job.

Footsteps sounded down the walk that led past his bench, and he drew deeper into the shadows. The steps slowed and a man moved to the other end of the bench. Duke drew heavily on his cigarette, tossed it away, and started to get up.

"Drink?" There was a hand holding a flask in front of him. He hesitated, then took it, and let a long slug run down his throat. In the faint light he could make out the face of Director Flannery. The man nodded. "Sorry I was out when you came, O'Neill. One of the guards saw you out here, so I came over."

"You should have been in," Duke said, handing the flask back. "I've changed my mind since reading about some of your deals in the *Journal*. Well, thanks for the drink."

One of Flannery's prosthetic hands rested on Duke's shoulder, and the pressure was surprisingly heavy. "When a man takes a drink with me, captain, he waits until I finish mine." He tipped up the flask and drank slowly before putting it away. "I suppose you mean the Cathay-Kloomiria mess?"

"What else?" Mess was a mild word. The Sugfarth ship had seemed to make victory for Cathay certain the first few days, but the war had entered a new phase now. Cathay couldn't maintain the big ship, and it was practically useless. It had simply served to reduce Kloomiria to a position where both sides were equal. The war showed signs of settling down to another prolonged, exhausting affair.

"Yeah, I read the editorial." Flannery sighed. "We did let a couple of fools make Cathay think we'd bail her out. At the time, it seemed wise. The son of old Var was due to assume rule in a little while and he was strongly pro-human. We wanted to hold things off until he took over and scrapped the war plans. When he was killed—well, we pulled out before Var was any stronger."

"And sent Queeth's crowd in to do your blood-letting for you?" Duke sneered.

"That was their own idea," Flannery denied. He lighted a cigarette and sat staring at the end of it, blowing out a slow stream of smoke. "All right, we made a mess of Cathay. We'll know better next time. Care to walk back with me?"

"Why? So one of your trained psychopropagandists can indoctrinate me? Or to get drunk and cry over your confession?"

"To keep me from sinking to your level and pushing your nose down your throat!" Flannery told him, but there was no real anger in his voice. He stood up, shrugging. "Nobody's forcing you, O'Neill. Say the word and I'll drive you home. But if you want that explanation, my working office seems like a good place to talk."

For a moment, Duke wavered. But he'd reached the end of his own research, and he'd come here to find the answers. Leaving now would only make him more of a fool. "O.K.," he decided. "I'll stay for the big unveiling."

Flannery grimaced. "There's no great secret, though we don't broadcast the facts for people and races not ready for them. We figure those who finish growing up here will soak up most of it automatically. Did you get around to the film file on interstellar wars at the library?"

Duke nodded, wondering how much they knew about his activities. He'd spent a lot of time going over the film for clues. It was so old that the color had faded in places. The rest would have been easier to take without color.

Most wasn't good photography, but all was vivid. It was the record of all the wars since Earth's invention of the high-drive—nearly two hundred of them. Gimsul, Hathor, Ptek, Sugfarth, Clovis, and even Meloa—the part he hadn't seen, beyond Kordule where the real damage lay; Ronda had been wrong, and cannibalism had been discovered, along with much that was worse. Two hundred wars in which victor and vanquished alike had been ruined—in which the supreme effort needed to win had left most of the victors worse than the defeated systems.

"War!" The word was bitter on Flannery's lips. "Someone starts building war power—power to insure peace, as they always say. Then other systems must have power to protect themselves. Strength begets force—and fear and hatred. Sooner or later, the strain is too great, and you have a war so horrible that its very horror makes surrender impossible. You saw it on Meloa. I've seen it fifty times!"

They reached the Foreign Office building and began crossing its lobby. Flannery glanced up at the big seal on the wall with its motto in twisted Latin—*Per Astra ad Aspera*—and his eyes turned back to Duke's, but he made no comment. He led the way to a private elevator that dropped them a dozen levels below the street, to a small room, littered with things from every conceivable planet. One wall was covered with what seemed to be the control panel of a spaceship, apparently now used for a desk. The director dropped into a chair and motioned Duke to another.

He looked tired, and his voice seemed older as he bent to pull a small projector and screen from a drawer and set them up. "The latest chapter of the film," he said bitterly, throwing the switch.

It was a picture of the breakup of the Outer Federation, and in some ways worse than the other wars. Chumkt rebelled against Kel's leadership and joined the aliens, while a civil war sprang up on her surface. Two alien planets went over to Kel. The original war was forgotten in a struggle for new combinations, and a thousand smaller wars replaced it. The Federation was dead and the two dozen races were dying.

"When everything else fails, the fools try federation," Flannery said as the film ended. "We tried it on Earth. Another race discovered the interstellar drive before we did and used it to build an empire. We've found the dead and sterile remains of their civilization. It's always the same. When one group unites its power, those nearby must ally for protection. Then there's a scramble for more power, while jealousies and fears breed new hatreds, internally and externally. And finally, there's ruin—because at the technological level of interstellar travel, victory in war is absolutely, totally impossible!"

He sat back, and Duke waited for him to resume, until it was obvious he had finished. At last, the younger man gave up waiting. "All right," he said. "Earth won't fight! Am I supposed to turn handsprings? I figured that much out myself. And I learned a long time ago about the blessed meek who were to inherit the Earth—but I can't remember anything being said about the stars!"

"You think peace won't work?" Flannery asked mildly.

"I know it won't!" Duke fumbled for a cigarette, trying to organize his thoughts. "You've been lucky so far. You've counted on the fact that war powers have to attack other powers nearby before they can safely strike against Earth, and you've buffered yourself with a jury-rigged economic trading system. But what happens when some really bright overlord decides to by-pass his local enemies? He'll drop fifty planet bombs out of your peaceful skies and collect your vassal worlds before they can rearm. You won't know about that, though. You'll be wiped out!"

"I wouldn't call our friends vassals, or say the system was jury-rigged," Flannery objected. "Ever hear of paradynamics? The papers call it the ability to manipulate relationships, when we let them write a speculative article. It's what lets us rebuild worlds in less than half a century—and form the first completely peaceful politico-economic culture we've ever known. Besides, I never said we had no weapons for our defense."

Duke considered it, trying to keep a firm footing on the shifting quicksand of the other's arguments. He knew a little of paradynamics, of course, but only as something supposed to remake the world and all science in some abstract future. It had been originated as a complex mathematical analysis of nuclear relationships, and had been seized on for some reason by the sociologists. It had no bearing he could see on the main argument.

"It won't wash, Flannery. Without a fleet, it won't matter if you have the plans of every weapon ever invented. The first time a smart power takes the chance, you'll run out of time."

"We didn't!" Flannery swung to the control board that served as his desk, and his fingers seemed to play idly with the dials. From somewhere below them, there was a heavy vibration, as if great engines had sprung into life. He pressed another switch.

Abruptly, the room was gone. There was a night sky above them, almost starless, and with a great, glaring moon shining down, to show a rough, mossy terrain that seemed covered endlessly with row after row of rusting, crumbling spaceships. Atomic cannon spilled from their hatches, and broken ramps led down to the ground. Down one clearer lane among the countless ships that surrounded him, Duke saw what might be a distant fire with a few bent figures around it, giving the impression of age.

FLANNERY

Beside him, Flannery sat in his chair, holding a small control. There was nothing else of the office visible.

The director shook his head. "It's no illusion, O'Neill. You're here—fifty odd thousand light-years from Earth, where we transferred the attacking fleet.

You never heard of that, of course. The dictator-ruler naturally didn't make a report when his fleet simply vanished without trace. Here!"

The liquor burned in Duke's throat, but it steadied him. He bent down, to feel the mossy turf under his hand.

"It's real," Flannery repeated. "Paradynamics handles all relationships, captain. And the position of a body is simply a statement of its geometrical relationships. What happens if we change those relationships—with power enough, that is? There is no motion, in any classic sense. But newspapers appear two high-drive days away minutes after they're printed. We arrive here. And fleets sent against Earth just aren't there any more!"

He pressed a button, and abruptly the walls of his office were around them again—the office that was suddenly the control room of a building that was more of a battleship than any Duke had ever seen.

He found himself clutching the chair, and forced himself to relax, soaking up the shock as he had soaked up so many others. His mind faced the facts, accepted them, and then sickly extended them.

"All right, you've got weapons," he admitted, and disgust was heavy in his voice. "You can defend yourself. But can the galaxy defend itself when somebody decides it's a fine offensive weapon? Or are all Earthmen supposed to be automatically pure, so this will never be turned to offensive use? Prove that to me and maybe I'll change my mind about this planet and take that job of yours!"

Flannery leaned back, nodding soberly. "I intend to," he answered. "Duke, we tried making peaceful citizens of our youngsters here a century ago, but it wouldn't work. Kids have to have their little gang wars and their fisticuffs to grow up naturally. We can't force them. Their interests aren't those of adults. In fact, they think adults are pretty dull. No adventure. They can't see that juggling a twenty-million gamble on tooling up for a new competitive product is exciting; they can't understand working in a dull laboratory to dig something new out of nature's files can be exciting and dangerous. Above all, they can't see that the greatest adventure is the job of bringing kids up to be other adults. They regret the passing of dueling and affairs of honor. But an adult civilization knows better—because the passing of such things is the first step toward a race becoming adult, because it is adopting a new type of thinking, where such things have no value. You didn't hit me when I called you names, because it made no sense from an adult point of view. Earth doesn't go to war for the same reason. Thank God, we grew up just before we got into space, where adult thinking is necessary to survival!"

There had been the kids and their seemingly pointless argument on the street. There had been the curiously distant respect the Meloans had shown him, as if they guessed that only his exterior was similar. There were a lot of things Duke could use to justify believing the director. It made a fine picture—as it was intended to.

"It must be wonderful to sit here safely, while agents do your dangerous work, feeling superior to anyone who shows any courage," he said bitterly. "I suppose every clerk and desk-jockey out there feeds himself the same type of rationalization. But words don't prove anything. How do you prove the difference between maturity and timidity or smugness?"

"You asked for it," Flannery said simply.

The button went down on the control again. The air was suddenly thin and bitingly cold as they looked down on a world torn with war, where a hundred ships shaped like half-disks and unlike anything Duke had seen were mixed up in some maneuver. The button was pushed again, and this time there was a world below that had a port busy with similar ships, not fighting now. A third press brought them onto the surface of a heavy world that seemed to be composed of solid buildings and factories, where the ships were being outfitted with incomprehensible goods. A thing like a pipe-stem man looked up from a series of operations, made a waving motion to them, and abruptly disappeared.

"Did you really think we could be the only adult race in the universe?" Flannery asked. "You're looking at the Allr, the closest cultural gestalt to us, and somewhere near our level. Now—"

Something squamous perched on a rock on what seemed to be a barren world. Before it floated bright points of light that were obviously replicas of planets, with tiny lines of light between them, and a shuttling of glints along the lines. The thing seemed to look at them, briefly. A tentacle whipped up and touched Flannery, who sat with his hands off the control box. Without its use, they were abruptly back in their office.

Flannery shivered, and there was strain on his face, while Duke felt his mind freeze slowly, as if with physical cold. The director cleared his throat. "Or maybe we should look at more routine things, though you might consider that we have to get ready for the day when our advancing culture touches on other cultures. Because we can't put it off forever."

This time, they were in a building, like a crude shed, and there were men there, standing in front of a creature that seemed like a human in armor— but chitinous armor that was part of him. The alien suddenly turned, though Duke could now see that they were in a section behind one-way glass. Nevertheless, it seemed to sense them. Abruptly, something began pulling at his mind, as if his thoughts were being drained. Flannery hit the button again. "Telepathic race, and very immature," he said, and there was worry in his voice. "Thank God, the only one we've found, and out of our immediate line of advance."

There were other scenes. A human being who walked endlessly three feet off the floor, fighting against some barrier that wasn't there, with his face frozen in fear, while creatures that seemed to be metallic moved about. "He found something while working on one of our paradynamic problems," Flannery said. "He transported himself there and has been exactly like that ever since—three years, now. So far, our desk-jockeys here haven't been able to discover exactly what line he was working on, but they're trying!"

They were back in the office, and the director laid the control box on the big panel and cut off the power. He swung back to face Duke, his face tired.

"You'll find a ship waiting to take you to Throm, and a man on board who'll use the trip to brief you, if you decide to take the job, Duke. As I said, it's up to you. If you still prefer your wars, come and see me next week, and maybe I can get the recruiting law set aside in your case, since you're really a citizen of Meloa. Otherwise, the ship takes off for Throm in exactly three hours."

He led the way back to the elevator, and rode up to the lobby. Duke moved out woodenly, but Flannery was obviously going no farther. The old man handed over what was left of the flask, shook Duke's hand quickly, and closed the elevator door.

Duke downed the liquor slowly, without thinking. Finally, a flicker of thought seemed to stir in his frozen mind. He shook himself and headed down the lobby toward the Earth outside. A faint vibration seemed to quiver in the air from below, and he quickened his steps.

Outside, he shook himself again, signaled a cab, and climbed in.

"The first liquor store you come to," he told the driver. "And then take me to the government space port, no matter what I say!"

X

It was quiet in the underground office of the director, except for the faint sound of Flannery's arms sliding across each other in an unconscious massaging motion. He caught himself at it, and leaned back, his tired facial muscles twitching into a faint smile.

Strange things happened to a man when he grew old. His hair turned gray, he thought more of the past, and prosthetic limbs began to feel tired, as if the nerves were remembering also. And the work that had once seemed vitally important in every detail winnowed itself down to a few things, with the rest only bothersome routine.

He pulled a thermos of coffee from under the desk and turned back to the confusion of red-coded memoranda on his desk. Then the sound of the elevator coming down caught his attention, and he waited until the door opened.

"Hello, Harding," he said without turning around. Only one man beside himself had the key to the private entrance. "Coffee?"

Harding took a seat beside him, and accepted the plastic cup. "Thanks. I tried to call you, but your phone was shut off. Heard the good word?"

Flannery shook his head. With the matter of the strange ship that had been reported and the problem of what to do with the telepaths both coming to a head, he'd had no time for casual calls. There was no question now that the telepaths had plucked the knowledge of how to build an interstellar drive from the observers' minds, in spite of all precautions. And once they broke out into the rest of the galaxy—

"Var died of a heart attack in the middle of a battle," Harding announced. "And Cathay and Kloomiria sent each other surrender notices the minute word was official! The damnedest thing I ever heard of. Edmonds came with me, and he's upstairs now, planning a big victory celebration as soon as we can let the word out. It should finish his reorientation."

"I'll probably get word on it by the time someone has it all organized into a nice, official memo," Flannery said. "Back him up on that celebration. It's worth a celebration to find out both worlds are that close to maturity. Coming over for bridge tonight?"

Harding shook his head. "I'll be up to my elbows in bills for the relief of Cathay and Kloomiria. It's a mess, even if it could be worse. Maybe tomorrow."

He dropped the cup onto the desk and turned to the elevator, while Flannery hunted through the memoranda. As he expected, he found a recent one announcing Var's death. He rubbed his arms together as he read it, but there was no new information in it.

Then, reluctantly, he picked up his phone and started to call. Scanning for information, just as another bundle of memos came through a small door in the panel. At the sight of the top photo, he put the phone back on its cradle. His face tautened and his arms lay limp as he read through it.

The picture was that of one of the half-disk Allr ships. The rumors of the strange ship were true enough. One of the Allr races had crossed the gulf between the two expanding cultures, and had touched several worlds briefly, to land in the biggest city on Ptek, the trading center for a whole sector. It had been there two days already, before being reported to Earth!

To make matters worse, it had come because its home world had been visited by a foreign ship—from the description, apparently from Sugfarth; there was no longer any chance of cutting off the news, since it would be circulating busily through both cultures. And with it must be going a thousand wild schemes by trading adventurers for exploration!

He'd expected it to happen some day, maybe in fifty years, after he was out of the office. By then enough of the worlds should have reached maturity to offer some hope of peaceful interpenetration. But now—

Victory, he thought bitterly. A small victory, and then this. Or maybe two small victories, if O'Neill worked out as well on Throm as he seemed to be doing, and if he realized he'd never be satisfied until he could return to Earth to face the problems he now knew existed. Flannery had almost hoped that it would be O'Neill who would handle the problem of cultural interpenetration. The man had ability.

But all that was in the past now, along with all the other victories. And in the present, as always, there were larger and larger problems, while full maturity lay forever a little farther on.

Then he smiled slowly at himself. There were problems behind him, too—ones whose solutions made these problems possible. And there would always be victory enough.

What was victory, after all, but the chance to face bigger and bigger problems without fear?

Flannery picked up the phone, and his arms were no longer tired.

THE END